Vindhyagatha

"An Epic of Faith"

Ayush Kumar Singh

This edition is the English translation of the original Hindi work titled, विन्ध्यगाथा ।

Declaration

This book is a work of fiction. All characters, places, events, and dialogues described in this book are the result of the author's imagination. Any resemblance to any living or deceased person, community, institution, or place is purely coincidental. The author's intention is not to hurt the sentiments of any individual or group.

Ayush Kumar Singh

01/10/2025

New Delhi

Vindhyagatha

Synopsis

Nestled within the dense forests and timeless mountains of the Vindhyachal range lies Vindhyagad—a small, cherished kingdom where the echoes of devotion, love, and valor resonate in every direction.

It was here that Princess Kaashvi was born, her heart brimming with devotion to Maa Durga and an infinite compassion for humanity. Her eyes held a radiant spark, yet the paths of life seemed to whisper that to claim love and freedom, she would have to wrestle with adversity.

Into her life one day steps Madhav, a young orphan whose simplicity, courage, and unblemished love touch the very depths of her soul. But the constraints of society and its rigid rules tear them apart.

This tale is a journey through their struggle, sacrifice, and devotion. From the confinements of the palace to the sanctum of the revered Shakti Peeth in Vindhyachal, the princess pours out the anguish of her heart, her unwavering faith, and her hopes in communion with Maa Vindhyavasini.

This novel transports you on a thrilling, spiritual, and deeply emotional voyage. where love and devotion intertwine to imbue life with profound meaning. With every page, the reader is gently reminded that this is not merely a story; it is a saga of life itself, one scripted by the divine hand of Maa Bhavani.

Author: Ayush Kumar Singh

1: Vindhyagadh

As the first rays of the rising sun touched the peaks of the Vindhyachal mountains in the east, it seemed as though a temple adorned in golden splendor had descended upon the earth. The golden aura spread slowly across the slopes of the mountain range, like a divine painter scattering colors upon nature's canvas. Below, the valleys covered in dense sal forests still lay asleep in the blue-tinted mist, but the summit had already received the day's message. A gentle fragrance permeated the air—a blend of wild jasmine, honey-bearing flowers, and some late-blooming winter blossoms, as if the flowers themselves had offered themselves in the arati of that sacred land. The melodious chirping of birds, which had earlier sounded like solitary notes, had now transformed into a collective hymn, celebrating the arrival of dawn.

This was Vindhyagadh, a small but prosperous kingdom of ancient India, a gem nestled in the lap of the Vindhyachal mountains, whose luster had spread far and wide. Its prosperity lay not merely in its treasures of gold and silver, but in its fertile soil, verdant forests, and ever-flowing rivers. The king who sat upon its throne, Maharaj Mahendra Pratap, was like a divine being incarnate. His name had become synonymous with justice, valor, and piety. Tales of his bravery were part of local lore. It was said that he had once single-handedly protected a merchant caravan surrounded by ten bandits. But even more renowned than his valor was his sense of justice. His subjects regarded him as a father, and he truly nurtured his kingdom like a family. The doors of his court were always open to the poor and the rich alike, and anyone could approach him with hope for justice.

Yet, amidst this prosperity and power, King Mahendra Pratap carried within his own life a profound emptiness—a void that, despite all material opulence, was always felt. This void had originated on the day when his beloved queen, Kaushalya Devi, had departed from this mortal world at the birth of the princess. Queen Kaushalya was not merely a queen;

she was the soul of the kingdom. Her sweet voice, her boundless compassion for the distressed, and the balance she brought to the king's life, these were qualities that elevated a ruler to even greater greatness. From that day onward, the conch shells of the palace, which once resonated daily with auspicious sounds morning and evening, had fallen silent. Laughter in the grand chambers of the palace had been replaced by a stillness, and the smile on the king's face seemed to have disappeared into the depths of some mountain. He still dispensed justice, managed state affairs, but the sparkle in his eyes, that vitality which the queen's presence had kindled within him, was gone.

As the sole, living memory of the queen, there grew up in the palace her daughter, Princess Kaashvi. Her name alone was enough to define her image, 'Kaashvi,' meaning 'the radiant one.' And truly, she radiance. Her face was as tender and divine as the full moon, like moonlight incarnate. In her large, kohl-rimmed eyes lay a remarkable depth and tranquility, like a clear, still lake. But her personality was far more extraordinary than her beauty. She was as deep as the ocean in her devotion. It was said that from childhood, she was an unwavering devotee of Maa Durga. While other princesses played with dolls and toys, Kaashvi's interest lay in the temple's conch shells, bells, and worship rituals. She would sit on the old stone steps of the temple, softly strumming her small veena and humming bhajans dedicated to Maa Vindhyavasini in her gentle voice. Maa Vindhyavasini, the goddess who resides in the Vindhyan mountains. This Jagdamba (Mother of the Universe) exists as the elder sister of Krishna; she had saved Krishna from Kamsa, she is the mother of the universe, and the most secret truth is that she is Krishna herself.

Kaashvi was raised by her caretaker, Sushila Devi, who was more than a mother to her. Sushila Devi herself had been Queen Kaushalya's most trusted confidante, and in the queen's absence, she became the very axis of Kaashvi's life. She was her guru, her protector, and her companion. Sushila Devi, whose hair was now gently graying and whose face bore the wrinkles of life's experiences, possessed an infinite well of patience and immeasurable love. It was she who would wake Kaashvi in the Brahma muhurta before dawn and take her to the inner temple of the palace for prayer, explaining to her, "Daughter, when the name of the Mother resides in the heart, no sorrow can endure. This world is an ocean, and the remembrance of the Mother is the only boat that can safely ferry you across every storm."

And Kaashvi had made these words the mantra of her life. Her days were adorned with a divine discipline. After the morning prayers, she would spend time studying Sanskrit and philosophy. Her teacher, Pandit Vishwambharnath, was often astonished by her intelligence and profound questions. The afternoons were dedicated to painting. Kaashvi had a great fondness for creating images of nature and the gods and goddesses. The walls of her chamber were decorated with her own paintings, on one side, a sunrise over the Vindhyachal; on another, various postures of Maa Durga. Every line that emerged from her brush seemed to carry a distinct energy of devotion.

Within the palace, tales of her devotion and divine nature had spread far and wide. People regarded her as 'the manifest grace of the Goddess.' Every evening, a grand arati ceremony for Maa Durga was held within the palace, preparations for which continued throughout the day. The palace's main temple would fill with the fragrance of gold and silver lamps, flowers, and incense. And King Mahendra Pratap himself would regularly attend this ceremony. He would sit to one side, observing his daughter immersed in the arati with complete devotion. When Kaashvi sang the arati hymns, her voice carried such sweetness and spiritual resonance that it would give listeners goosebumps. In those moments, King Mahendra Pratap's eyes would glisten with a peculiar light, a complex mixture of emotions. On one hand, there was immense pride in his daughter; on the other, a sharp pang of memory for Queen Kaushalya. The same question would flicker in his eyes every time: "Is this the image of my Queen Kaushalya? Is this her legacy, manifesting before me in this form?"

The king, who had found profound sorrow entering his life with the birth of his daughter, was now rediscovering faith and the meaning of life in that very daughter. Kaashvi was not merely a daughter to him; she was a thread connecting him to the queen. Sometimes, when Kaashvi wore the queen's old jewelry on special occasions, or spoke in a manner reminiscent of her, the king would feel as though time had paused for a few moments. He would gaze at her, and while an ocean of affection for his daughter would swell in his heart, on the other hand, a pang would also arise, the pang of life without that companion who could not share all this with him.

This dawn in Vindhyagadh, which arrived each day bearing the message of a new light, was not merely the beginning of another day. It was the prelude to a saga destined to weave the complex threads of love, devotion, and destiny in the times to come. This was the saga of a princess whose faith was to lead her to a crossroads where she would have to choose between her belief, her duty, and her heart. This was the saga of a king who, having lost everything and found it again, was now to face another trial. And this was the saga of a kingdom whose destiny was unknowingly intertwined with the devotion of a young princess and the fatherhood of a king. The sun had now fully risen, and Vindhyagadh had awakened. But within this awakening, there was also an unspoken anticipation, the anticipation of a story yet to be written.

2: A New Stirring

As time passed, Kaashvi had entered her adolescence. The tender lines of childhood were now beginning to take on the definite contours of youth, yet her eyes still held the same purity as in childhood, but now an unfamiliar depth also reflected in them. A depth filled not merely with questions, but with unspoken answers. Her mornings still began with the arati of Maa Durga. The dawn hours would fill the palace with a special kind of peace and spiritual energy. As she walked toward the temple, her gentle footsteps would echo through the halls, and then, with the sweet resonance of bells, the fragrance of camphor, the flame of the lamp, and her slow, heartfelt prayers, the entire palace would become suffused with a wondrous radiance. This was not merely a ritual; it was a living experience that breathed life into the stones of the palace.

The delicacy of adolescence had blossomed on Kaashvi's face; the innocent laughter of childhood remained, but now it carried a new edge, an unfamiliar longing, a soft touch that words could not express. Her mornings were the same: worship at the feet of Maa Vindhyavasini, running her fingers along the necks of the lamps, and sitting on the temple steps singing gentle hymns. But this time, something was different. From some corner of her eyes, she would gaze into the distance, and even amidst laughter, she would fall into thought, as if the final word of a song remained unsung.

King Mahendra Pratap remained attentive toward his daughter. He was not only her teacher but also expressed concern over every small matter concerning her. But Kaashvi's caretaker, Sushila Devi, had been giving her motherly affection since childhood.

The palace garden was Kaashvi's second temple of devotion. This was no ordinary garden; it was a vibrant hermitage of colors and fragrances. Jasmine, roses, champaka, and rare flowers brought from the valleys of the Vindhyachal always bloomed here in abundance. For Kaashvi, every bud seemed like an offering from Maa Durga, every blossoming flower a symbol of her grace. She would come to stroll in this garden daily after sunrise, seeking the Mother's vision in this temple of nature.

An elderly gardener came there every day. Mahesh Das, who had served the royal palace for generations. Time had etched lines on his face, but his hands were still so skilled that flowers seemed to freshen at his touch. Every morning, he would pluck the freshest and most fragrant flowers, then meditate as he strung them into garlands, which Kaashvi would directly offer at the feet of the Mother in the temple.

Kaashvi would smile at him daily and ask, "Kaka, which flower garland will please Mother today?"

This was their daily ritual, a sacred game. Mahesh Das would reply with a laugh, "Daughter, Mother seeks the heart's emotion; flowers are merely an excuse. Your pure heart is the true garland that pleases her."

But one cold morning, something was different. An unusual stillness hung in the air. Kaashvi arrived at the garden, but the familiar, affectionate voice that greeted her was not heard. A fresh basket of flowers lay on the stone platform, but Mahesh Das was nowhere to be seen. A strange emptiness enveloped her. She looked around, and then Sushila Devi appeared there, faint lines of concern on her face.

Kaashvi asked in a soft, uncertain voice, "Dai Maa, Kaka did not come today?"

Sushila Devi took a deep breath and explained, "Daughter, Mahesh Kaka is very ill. Fever, joint pain. He is aged; his body is failing him. Someone else will bring the flowers today in his place."

A liquid concern welled up in Kaashvi's heart. Mahesh Kaka was a steady, reliable part of her life. His absence created an unfamiliar imbalance. She asked, her voice carrying even softer gravity, "Someone else?"

"Yes, daughter," Sushila Devi explained, "his disciple, his name is Madhav. He will bring the flowers from today, until Kaka recovers."

It was evening time. The sun was descending toward the western mountains, and the sky was blending golden and orange hues. Lamps had begun to flicker in the temple courtyard, their soft, shimmering light spreading a divine canopy over the entire atmosphere. Kaashvi stood at the temple door when she first saw him.

Then, on the garden path, a simple young man appeared. He wore an ordinary cotton dhoti, yet the soil and flower-color stains on his garments seemed like hues on an artist's clothes. His body was well-formed and sinewy, reflecting strength cultivated through hard labor. But his true beauty resided in his face and features. His complexion bore a wheatish tone, upon which the sun had scattered a golden glow. His nose was straight and sharp, his lips sensitive and slightly curved, as if always concealing a gentle, unspoken smile.

But his eyes... his eyes were as calm and deep as a still lake. They were large and kohl-rimmed, and they held an extraordinary radiance, the kind of radiance that finds its way even through darkness, like stars in the night sky. In those eyes reflected a wondrous peace and thoughtfulness, as if he understood the profound mysteries of nature and life. In his hands was a beautiful garland of jasmine and roses, and his feet were stained with dust, testament to the long distance from the garden. Yet his gait carried such grace, dignity, and rhythm that he seemed like a seeker, not merely a gardener's assistant, but a disciplined priest of nature.

He advanced silently, gathering even the sound of his footsteps. His gaze was on the ground, bowed in a kind of deep humility, yet an indomitable confidence radiated from his very being. He placed the garland near the threshold of the temple and, joining his palms, offered a deep, heartfelt obeisance, first toward the sanctum sanctorum, and then, with a natural gesture, toward Kaashvi.

Seeing him, Kaashvi's mind seemed to pause for a moment. Not merely the attractiveness of his form, but the spontaneous and sacred aura pervading his entire image added a new note to her devotional song. The young man placed the garland, greeted her in a soft voice, and departed. Kaashvi did not learn his name at that moment; more than his name, it was the impact of his face. An unspoken, gentle, profound effect that spread like a ripple in the still lake of her mind.

And then, an indescribable event occurred. Kaashvi's heart seemed to stop for an instant. A strange warmth spread across her cheeks. She received garlands daily; this ritual was an ordinary part of her daily life. But today, something new, unfamiliar, and intense vibrated within her. It was not fear, nor merely curiosity. It was a sensation as if an ancient, forgotten melody had suddenly begun to play in the air. She picked up the garland, and for a moment her gaze lifted toward the young man, who had already turned and was walking away. Looking at his back, she felt a strange emptiness.

When night returned from the temple threshold, Kaashvi sat near the lamp. In the gentle breeze, the resonance of bells, the fragrance of the garland, and the memory of that strange commotion all combined to create an uncanny reverberation within her. But she told no one; Kaashvi knew that matters of the palace could not remain within walls. So she transformed her anguish into prayer, surrendering everything at the Mother's feet.

That night, Kaashvi sat in the temple for a long time before the Mother. The lamp flame flickered, its shadows performing a mysterious dance on the walls. Gazing at the peaceful, compassionate face of the Mother's idol, she asked in her mind, "Mother, what is this commotion within me today? What is this unrest? This person is a stranger, so why does his coming and going stir ripples in the still lake of my mind?"

The Mother's idol remained silent, as always. But then, even in the absence of a strong gust of wind, the lamp flame trembled, flickered. Kaashvi saw it, and she felt that the answer was there too—not in words, but in experience, in this vibration. This silent answer unsettled her even more.

As the day passed, her four friends—Tara Kumari, Vijaya, and Lakshika, gathered in the same garden where they often played. Kaashvi's steps were light, but there was a certain flush in her eyes. The friends immediately sensed that something was new. Then came what always did: laughter, chatter, and those sweet, heart-touching moments of teasing that become songs in young girls' hearts.

Tara Kumari said laughingly, "Kaashvi, today you seem completely lost in dreams! Has some prince stolen you away?"

Kaashvi smiled quickly but blushed, "You people! Don't joke."

Vijaya, who was sensible but never behind in mischief, spoke up. "We saw you came late from the temple. And that new gardener? There must be something, tell us."

Lakshika widened her eyes. "Color has come to your cheeks, has someone bound flowers for you?"

Tara said with a laugh, "If it is a matter of honey (Madhav), then all three of us together will put him to the test, we'll see how much courage he has!"

Kaashvi hesitated, then said, "You all, I'm just playing. Why spread any matter so quickly?"

Vijaya said in a lowered voice, "But Princess, we understand what passes secretly through the heart. Whenever you want, we are here."

There was laughter in their words, but sweetness too. They sat quietly by the lotus pond and hummed old tales, sometimes discussions of palace weddings, sometimes chasing after fluttering butterflies. But in between, they kept returning to ask about that young man, his steps, his humility, and that strange peace. Kaashvi would say something each time and then fall silent; but her friend's words kept opening the echoes of her heart further.

Finally, Tara sighed and said, "Come, tomorrow we will all together linger on the path from which that gardener came. If he comes again, we will see him."

Vijaya nodded, "But carefully, the palace has eyes everywhere."

Lakshika gently took Kaashvi's hand and said, "We are together, no matter what."

From that day on, Kaashvi's eyes began, unintentionally, without any conscious effort, to search for that one face. Whenever she went to the garden, or entered the temple, her gaze would automatically travel to the path from which Madhav would appear. Sometimes she would see him from a distance, picking flowers, his carefulness, his gentle touch toward the blooms. She did not know why all this was happening. She did not know that destiny had, in that ordinary moment, tied the first thread of her and Madhav's life-leelas, a thread destined to be woven into the complex fabric of love, devotion, and duty in the times to come.

That night, as they all parted, a soft trust took root in Kaashvi's heart, that the king's boundaries might change, but perhaps in the pathways of destiny, a change in tone does sometimes occur. And with that faith, the path turned toward the future.

3: The Sprouting of Love

The sunrises over Vindhyagadh were no longer as they once were. Earlier, when the sun's rays bathed the mountain peaks, it seemed as though nature herself was performing the arati of Maa Vindhyavasini. Now, those same golden rays brought for Kaashvi a new hope, an unspoken anticipation. When Kaashvi went to the temple in the morning, her steps no longer held their former innocence, now every footstep reflected an invisible waiting. She would walk toward the temple, but her gaze would wander toward the garden, where a fragrance and an image had taken residence in her heart.

A sweet breeze blew through the palace garden, but within her there was another scent. The scent of a name that had now slowly sprouted in her memories: Madhav. That name was no longer merely a word but had become a heartbeat within her. Whenever she repeated that name silently to herself, she felt as though a sweet melody had begun to play within her.

After that first meeting, he would often come carrying the basket of flowers, and each time Kaashvi felt as though time had paused for a few moments. She had begun to recognize his sweet footfall from a distance. The sound of his steps was neither heavy nor light, but carried a balanced rhythm, as if nature herself were walking. When he drew near, Kaashvi's heart would begin to beat with a strange quickening. She would smile at small things, ask questions, sometimes about the colors of the garland, sometimes about the name of a rare flower.

"Madhav, why is this jasmine so fragrant today?" she would ask, though her heart said, 'The fragrance of your arrival is even more enchanting than this.'

"Perhaps the coolness after the rain has enhanced their essence, Princess," Madhav would reply with humility, his gaze lowered.

But behind her questions lay another reason. An excuse to meet, an opportunity to see. Every question was a door that opened her a little more toward him. Every answer was a window through which she caught a glimpse of his soul.

Madhav, who was of simple and humble nature, initially considered these interactions as the princess's natural grace. He would think, it is a princess's duty to behave kindly toward her servants. But gradually, he too began to sense that a soft vibration lay hidden in these meetings, a touch that was beyond words. When he looked into her eyes, a mixture of fear and joy would course through him; and when she lowered her gaze, it seemed as though some mystery had just been born. He tried to convince his mind: 'This is merely an illusion, a dream that will shatter.' But what his heart was feeling was no illusion; it was a truth that had become woven into his existence.

Days passed. Sometimes she would come near him while he was picking flowers in the garden, sometimes she would stop on the temple steps on some pretext. One day, as Madhav was gathering rose buds, Kaashvi arrived there.

"Do you think these roses should be plucked before they bloom?" she asked.

Madhav looked, there was a deep question in her eyes. "No, Princess. Every flower should have the opportunity to bloom. Until its petals have fully opened, its fragrance and beauty are not complete."

"But sometimes the gardener knows when to pluck which flower," Kaashvi said, smiling.

Madhav bowed his head. "But the gardener is only a servant, Princess. Flowers are nature's gift, and there is no gardener greater than nature."

Only ordinary sentences were exchanged between them, but behind them surged an ocean of emotions. Every word carried a meaning, every silence was a dialogue. They were two different streams, slowly flowing toward the same sea.

One morning, when soft sunlight spread all around and dewdrops sparkled on the roses, Kaashvi gathered courage. That night she had thought: 'Why not? Why should I not ask him what lies in my heart? Does being a princess mean I must suppress my feelings?'

She reached that corner of the garden where Madhav was arranging flowers in a basket. At that spot was a jasmine creeper whose fragrance permeated the entire atmosphere. Madhav was seated on a stone platform, holding freshly plucked roses and jasmine flowers in his hands. He was so absorbed that he didn't even sense Kaashvi's arrival.

Kaashvi stood silently for a few moments, admiring the skill of his hands. Then she spoke in a soft voice: "Madhav, do you think of me only as a princess?"

Madhav froze. The flowers stopped in his hands. He raised his head, and in his eyes were expressions of astonishment and some fear. His voice trembled as he replied: "You are a princess, divine-like. I am merely a servant. My duty is to respect you."

Kaashvi smiled, but her eyes said something else. Those eyes, which usually remained so calm and serious, today spoke a different language.

"Being a princess is destiny's constraint, Madhav. It is a mantle that has been draped upon me. But hearts are the same in everyone. There is no distinction of high and low within them. Do you think a princess's heart is made of stone, like the walls of her palace?"

Madhav looked at her, for the first time directly, without fear, without hesitation. In that gaze was astonishment, fear, and a deep compassion. He knew how dangerous this conversation was, but his eyes could not deny the truth that shone clearly in Kaashvi's eyes.

He said in a trembling voice: "Princess, please do not say this. You know what society we live in. If the king comes to know, I will have to lose my life. Your place and my place, this is a chasm that can never be bridged. Our worlds are different. Your sky is high, and I can never reach that height. I am an ordinary person of the earth, and you... you are like a goddess of heaven."

Moisture came to Kaashvi's eyes. She took a step forward, and her voice held a firmness that had never been there before.

"But does love need any height, Madhav? Are feelings bound by any limits? Love is what binds earth and sky together. When I am with you, I feel I am coming to know myself. In your presence, I am only Kaashvi. An ordinary woman, an ordinary heart."

A storm arose within Madhav. His mind was divided into two parts, on one side was his duty, warning him; on the other side was his heart, agreeing with every word Kaashvi said. He knew this path was fraught with dangers, but the truth in Kaashvi's eyes drew him toward her.

"Princess," he said in a pained voice, "what you are saying sounds very beautiful. But reality is not so beautiful. I am a disciple of a poor gardener. I have neither wealth nor status. Your father, Maharaj Mahendra Pratap, will never accept this relationship. And if he becomes angry, then not only my life, but my guru Mahesh Das's life too will be in danger. Do you want someone's life to be endangered because of me?"

Kaashvi took a deep breath. "I do not want to put anyone in danger, Madhav. But do you think true love does not rise above all these constraints? I have prayed to Maa Vindhyavasini, and I believe she will guide us."

Madhav bowed his head. What more could he say? He had no answer. He picked up the basket of garlands and left without saying anything. But his steps no longer held their former firmness. He felt broken, disturbed, caught in a conflict of emotions.

After that day, he did not come for many days. Kaashvi would go to the garden, but found only empty paths and silent buds. The flower basket was now brought by another servant, an elderly person who would place the basket and leave without speaking.

The first day, Kaashvi thought: 'Perhaps he is busy with some work.' The second day, she thought: 'Perhaps he is occupied serving Mahesh Kaka.' On the third day, when she still did not see Madhav, a restlessness began to spread in her mind, sometimes anger, sometimes anxiety, and sometimes the belief that he would return.

Sitting in her chamber, she would think: 'Did I make a mistake? Should I not have said all this to him?' But then she would feel that whatever she had said was true. The feelings her heart held for Madhav were not false in any way.

One day, as she sat praying in the temple, tears streamed from her eyes. "Mother," she said in her mind, "is loving a sin? Cannot a princess's heart be so free that she can choose her feelings? I have always worshipped you, dedicated my life to you. Will you not support me in this love?"

At that moment, a lamp in the temple flickered brightly, as if giving an answer. Kaashvi took this as an auspicious sign, and hope was rekindled in her heart.

Within the walls of the royal palace, her mind was no longer confined. She knew she had felt something that is life's truest experience. Love, which had sprouted, now needed the sunlight of courage to survive. And that courage was awakening within her.

She remained silent even before her friends Tara, Vijaya, and Lakshmi. They understood her state of mind, but now they did not speak openly on this subject. They knew this was no light matter. The princess's future was at stake.

One evening, when all the friends gathered in the garden, Tara said softly, "Kaashvi, you have been very quiet these days. Is everything alright?"

Kaashvi took a deep breath. "Everything is fine, Tara. It's just that sometimes life brings us to such crossroads where we must listen to our hearts, no matter how difficult it may be."

Vijaya looked at her with wise eyes. "We are with you, Kaashvi. Whatever happens, we will not leave you alone."

Lakshmi held her hand. "Your heart is pure, Kaashvi. Maa Vindhyavasini will guide you."

These words strengthened Kaashvi. She felt she was not alone.

And this was the moment when Kaashvi's heart first understood that being a princess was not a blessing but a test. A test of managing her feelings, her dignity, and her love, all together.

One night, when the moon was full and its moonlight spread across the palace courtyard, Kaashvi stood on her balcony. She looked toward the sky, and then toward the distant garden where Madhav used to come. She resolved that she would not give up. She would meet Madhav again, and this time she would make him understand that love is greater than any constraint.

But simultaneously, she also knew she would have to be careful. Within the palace walls, everyone was watching. Servants, officials, and perhaps the king himself. She had to find a way to meet Madhav without arousing anyone's suspicion.

She formed a plan. The next day, she would tell Dai Sushila that she wished to inquire about Mahesh Das's health and would go to see him. Under this pretext, she could meet Madhav.

When she made this plan, a peace settled in her mind. She knew this was only a small step, but it was a beginning. A beginning that could lead her toward her heart's desire.

That night, Kaashvi could not sleep. She kept thinking about her future, on one side was her love, on the other her duty. But she felt these two were not opposed to each other. If her love was pure and selfless, it could assist her in fulfilling her duties.

When morning came, Kaashvi resolved firmly that she would listen to her heart's voice, whatever the consequences. She knew this path would be difficult, but she had learned to trust in Maa Vindhyavasini. And with that faith, she stepped toward a new day, a day destined to write a new chapter in her life.

4: Struggle and Rebellion

The elderly gardener Mahesh Das, who had served the royal palace for generations, had fallen ill. With age, his body had begun to fail him, and the arrival of winter had intensified his sufferings. As Kaashvi had planned, she sought permission to care for Mahesh Das. It appeared as a natural desire, a gesture of compassion toward a loyal servant. But within her lay another feeling, another reason for going there. She knew that Madhav, Mahesh Das's disciple, would be engaged in his care.

King Mahendra Pratap gave his consent with affection. "Your heart is very generous, my daughter," he said, "but remember, you are a princess. Have compassion for servants, but maintain proper distance as well."

Kaashvi bowed her head and replied, "As you command, Pita shri." But a storm was rising in her heart. She knew that what she was about to do would violate that proper distance.

When she reached the gardener's dwelling, she saw the old man lying on his cot, and attending to him was that same young man, Madhav. Mahesh Das's home was a simple hut, with earthen walls and a thatched roof. But that day, that hut seemed to Kaashvi no less than any palace.

In Madhav's hands was medicine, on his face was fatigue, but in his eyes shone that same sweet radiance that had sprouted in Kaashvi's heart upon first seeing him. He was gently administering medicine to Mahesh Das, and there was such tenderness in his touch that Kaashvi's heart melted.

Kaashvi asked in a soft voice, "How is Mahesh Kaka now?"

Madhav bowed his head and said, "There is improvement now, Princess. By the grace of Maa Vindhyavasini, he will recover soon."

Around them were two other servants assisting in Mahesh Das's care. Kaashvi smiled and said, "You all go outside and bring fresh water and some medicine. I wish to stay with Kaka for a while."

The servants bowed and left. Now only two souls remained, and a silent atmosphere. Mahesh Das was in deep sleep, so he was not witness to this conversation.

Madhav lowered his gaze. "Princess, why have you come here? Seeing you in this hut fills me with fear. If someone has seen you... both your reputation and mine are at stake."

Kaashvi interrupted, "Why do you fear, Madhav? I have not come to break any rule, but to understand a truth. Is love a crime? Is it a sin for a woman to listen to the voice of her heart?"

Madhav's lips trembled. He said, "Not a crime, Princess, but in this world, it has been deemed a sin. If the king comes to know, my life will be destroyed. I had already told you this."

Kaashvi remained silent for a few moments, then spoke: "Then let us ask Father himself. If he gives his consent, you will have no fear. I will place the truth before him and tell him that my heart beats for you."

Madhav said softly, "If there were a place in his heart, perhaps I could even reach the palace gates. But Princess, the reality is the opposite. King Mahendra Pratap holds his reputation and family honor supreme. Forgive me. Do not come here again. We both must save ourselves from this fire."

Tears welled up in Kaashvi's eyes. "Madhav, is there nothing for me in your heart? Do I hold no place in your eyes, like an ordinary woman?"

Madhav did not answer, but his gaze said everything. It was filled with love, but bound by constraints. In his eyes was a deep pain, a struggle that was beyond words.

Kaashvi said softly, "In your silence itself lies the answer, Madhav. But if society wishes to imprison love, I will not remain silent. I will not hide this truth."

She rose, placed her hand affectionately on Mahesh Das's head, and walked toward the palace. Madhav looked at her, in his eyes was fear, and in his heart, fire. He knew that something was now about to happen, and he could not stop it.

That evening, Kaashvi returned to the royal palace and went straight to the royal court. The court chamber was vast, with images of ancient warriors and deities carved into its walls. King Mahendra Pratap was seated there, absorbed in matters of state. Gravity was on his face, and in his eyes reflected his devotion to the kingdom.

Taking a deep breath, Kaashvi said, "Pita-shri, I must tell you a truth."

The king raised his head. "What is it, putri? Why are you so serious?"

"Pita-shri," she said in a firm voice, "I have felt affection in my heart for someone. For a young man named Madhav."

The king lifted his head, in his gaze were both astonishment and anger. "What did you say?" His voice echoed against the palace walls. "Love for a servant's son? Kaashvi, this is an insult to our lineage! You must forget this."

Kaashvi's tears transformed into determination in her voice. "Pita-shri, love does not see caste or lineage. It is that same divine light that flows from the feet of Maa Vindhyavasini. Madhav is an ordinary young man, but his heart is pure, and his thoughts are noble. Is this not enough?"

The king thundered, "Enough now! You are not permitted to utter another word on this subject. You are a princess, and your marriage will be into a royal family. If you maintain any relation with that young man, you will no longer be my daughter."

Kaashvi bowed, but on her lips was the fire of silence. She spoke softly, "Say what you will, but I cannot betray my heart. If being a princess means suppressing my feelings, then I am ready to renounce this position."

Hearing this, the king's anger flared even more. "You will regret your words, putri. Now go to your chamber, and never discuss this subject again."

Kaashvi bowed once more and walked out of the royal court. In her heart was a strange peace. She had spoken the truth, and now she was ready for the consequences.

That night, Kaashvi reached the temple. The temple's atmosphere was calm and sacred. Before the idol of Maa Vindhyavasini, a lamp was burning, and in its flame flickered a divine radiance. With eyes moist with tears, Kaashvi gazed at the idol and spoke:

"Mother, is love also a sin? Is it wrong for a woman to listen to the voice of her heart? If this feeling is given by you, then I cannot abandon it. Show me the path. Tell me what I should do."

The lamp flame wavered, as if touched by an invisible hand. Kaashvi took this as a sign. She made a vow: "I can no longer remain within the walls of this palace. Where constraints prevent love from breathing, to remain there is adharma (unrighteousness). I will leave this palace today itself."

She decided to spend the night in the temple itself. Sitting before the Mother's idol, she became absorbed in meditation. Many thoughts arose in her mind, her father's anger, Madhav's fear, and her own future. But amidst all this, she experienced an inner strength. She knew she was on the right path.

The next day at dawn, when the entire palace was asleep, Kaashvi silently removed her jewelry, donned simple clothes, and moved toward the door. She prepared a small bundle containing only a few essential items. She knew that now her life would be spent in simplicity and the pursuit of truth.

She walked away from the palace, beyond the city, onto that forest path where there was the shade of trees and the melody of springs. Her steps were firm, and in her heart was an indomitable courage. She knew this path would be difficult, but she had no regret about her decision.

As Kaashvi walked, when her feet began to ache with fatigue and her breath grew heavy, suddenly, amidst the dense forest, the spire of an ancient temple showed her the way. That spire was so tall it seemed to be conversing with the sky itself, and upon it was inscribed the name 'Maa Vindhyavasini.' The temple walls had become dilapidated from the onslaughts of time, yet they possessed a wondrous divine aura. It seemed as though the Mother's grace itself had bestowed immortality upon these stones.

Kaashvi entered the temple with reverence and, standing before the idol, joined her palms: "Mother, if the world has rejected me, will your lap accept me? Will you support me in this struggle of mine?"

Just then, the temple bell rang of its own accord, without any touch, and its sweet sound sanctified the entire atmosphere. Kaashvi took this as the Mother's blessing, and a wonderful peace descended upon her heart. Indeed, the Mother is the ocean of compassion, if the world has rejected someone, who else but the Mother remains?

As she sat absorbed in meditation in the temple courtyard, she felt as though Maa Vindhyavasini herself had appeared before her and was saying: "Fear not, daughter. Your courage and your love will make you victorious."

After this divine experience, Kaashvi decided that she would remain in this temple and serve the Mother. But little did she know that this was no ordinary temple, but rather that same mythological site where Maa Vindhyavasini, in her eight-armed form, had appeared to Kamsa and protected Lord Shri Krishna.

This was that sacred land where the Mother manifests in her complete form before her devotees.

Kaashvi had no idea that in a cave behind the temple, Maharshi Advaitanand was absorbed in deep penance. He had been residing at this place for hundreds of years, worshipping the Mother. When Kaashvi arrived at the temple, the Maharshi's meditative state was broken, and through his divine vision, he came to know everything. He knew that this was the princess of Vindhyagadh, but he did not immediately reveal anything.

When Kaashvi had the darshan of the Maharshi and sought refuge from him, lines of compassion bloomed on his face. The Maharshi spoke: "Daughter, this place is always open for those who walk the path of truth. The courage you have shown is not ordinary. You may stay here without any worry."

From that day onward, under the guidance of Maharshi Advaitanand, Kaashvi dedicated her life to the devotion of Maa Vindhyavasini. She had faith that one day, not only Madhav but all of Vindhyagadh would understand the significance of her decision.

And thus began that chapter of Kaashvi's life which tells the immortal saga of love, courage, and faith, a saga destined to shake the foundations of Vindhyagadh in the times to come.

5: Chandi paath

Silence pervaded the ancient temple situated amidst the dense forests of the Vindhyachal. The idols of gods and goddesses carved on the temple walls had faded with time, yet a divine aura still resided within them. Princess Kaashvi—no, now the ascetic Kaashvi, sat absorbed in meditation before the eight-armed idol of Maa Vindhyavasini in the temple's sanctum.

A month had passed, but the storm in her mind showed no signs of subsiding. The renunciation of the royal palace's comforts and luxuries, the harshness of her father Mahendra Pratap, and the anguish of her love for Madhav, all these emotions kept rising and falling within her mind. Though she had sought refuge at the Mother's feet, inner peace still remained distant.

It was evening time. Seated on the temple steps, Kaashvi gazed at the distant Vindhyachal mountain range. The crimson of sunset was spreading an ethereal beauty over the mountains. Just then, a gentle voice echoed from behind: "Daughter, this silence is breaking you from within. You need not just devotion, but understanding as well."

Kaashvi turned to look. An elderly brahmin stood there, from whose countenance flowed an extraordinary radiance. In his eyes lay infinite depth, and on his face were lines of compassion. He was Maharshi Advaitanand.

"Maharshi!" Kaashvi bowed with reverence.

The Maharshi said affectionately, "I know the pain in your heart, but know this, this pain itself is the stairway to sadhana. I will tell you a story, which is not merely the tale of the Goddess, but the story of the mind, and within it lies the solution for how to fight with the mind."

In a corner of the temple, beneath a banyan tree, Maharshi Advaitanand seated himself. Directly before him, her head bowed in reverence, sat Kaashvi.

The Maharshi began in his calm voice: "My child Kaashvi, today I will narrate to you that sacred tale which destroys all mental afflictions. But before that, you should know the story of King Surath and the merchant Samadhi."

"Once upon a time, King Surath was defeated in battle. His entire kingdom was taken from him; his own people abandoned him. Yet, his mind remained obsessed with his lost kingdom, his palace, his horses. He could not understand why his mind was so agitated for a kingdom and wealth that no longer belonged to him. At the same time, there was a Vaishya, Samadhi. His sons and wife had robbed him of all his wealth and cast him out. Yet, he had no concern for his lost riches. He remained constantly anxious about his family, and was bewildered that even after losing everything, he could not cultivate detachment.

Both took shelter in the ashram of Rishi Medha. Through the sage's grace, every animal and bird there had knowledge of the ultimate truth. They were both troubled as to why they had not yet attained wisdom.

Then they approached Rishi Medha with their respective sorrows. The sage explained to them: 'O children! This is all the influence of Mahamaya. This same Mahamaya envelops the entire world and binds creatures in bondage. When she is pleased, she also grants liberation.' Then Rishi Medha narrated to them that sacred tale of the Devi Mahatmya which I am about to recount to you."

The Maharshi began the tale in a solemn voice:

"My child Kaashvi, at the dawn of creation, when the waters of dissolution pervaded the entire cosmos, Lord Vishnu lay immersed in yogic slumber on the serpent Shesha. In that divine sleep, he held the entire creation within himself.

Then a wondrous event occurred. From the wax in Lord Vishnu's ears, two mighty demons emerged, Madhu and Kaitabha. They were so powerful that their radiance made the entire submerged cosmos tremble.

At that time, Brahma was seated on his lotus throne. He saw the two demons advancing to attack him.

Terrified, Brahma realized that Vishnu, the protector, was in deep sleep.

Then Brahma prayed to that Goddess who is the embodiment of sleep itself:

'O Goddess! You are the form of Shiva, the form of peace, salutations to you. O Mahadevi! You are the refuge of all. O embodiment of Vishnu's sleep, bestower of boons, worshipped by the gods! Salutations to you. You are the consciousness of this world, you are the supreme goddess.'

Pleased with Brahma's praise, the Goddess appeared. Her form was supremely divine and radiant. She assured Brahma and then entered Vishnu's heart and awakened him. Lord Vishnu awoke and challenged Madhu and Kaitabha to battle. The fierce war continued for five thousand years. The demons had received a boon that they could not be killed anywhere where water existed."

The Maharshi continued the tale engagingly:

"When Vishnu could not defeat the demons, the Goddess suggested a stratagem. Vishnu said to the demons, 'Strike me in a place where there is no water.' Drunk with pride, the demons made the same promise to Vishnu. Then Vishnu placed them on his thigh and severed their heads from their bodies, for the entire cosmos was submerged and only his thigh was dry. Thus Madhu and Kaitabha were slain."

The Maharshi looked at Kaashvi and said:

"Child, understand the deep mystery of this story. Madhu and Kaitabha are symbols of the ignorance within us. Madhu represents sweetness, the worldly pleasures that bind us. Kaitabha represents fear, the dread that prevents us from moving forward. Vishnu is our consciousness, and the Goddess is that divine power that leads us out of the darkness of ignorance. When we take refuge in the Goddess, our consciousness awakens and we are able to slay the demons of ignorance within us."

The Maharshi continued the narrative:

"In later times, there arose a mighty demon named Mahishasura. Through severe penance, he pleased Lord Brahma. Brahma granted him the boon that no god, demon, human, or animal could kill him. Mahishasura became filled with arrogance. He attacked heaven, defeated Indra, and seized control of the heavens. The gods had to flee heaven, becoming homeless. The helpless gods approached Brahma, Vishnu, and Mahesh and narrated their plight. They said:

'O trinity! Mahishasura has taken control of all three worlds. We have been driven out of heaven. Protect us!'

Then Brahma, Vishnu, and Mahesh consoled the gods, and from the combined radiance of all of them, a wondrous light appeared."

The Maharshi described in a divine voice:

"From that light, an extraordinary Goddess manifested. Her face was radiant as the moon, her eyes brilliant as the sun. She had eighteen arms and was mounted on a lion.

All the gods gave her their respective weapons:

· Shiva gave his trident

· Vishnu gave his Sudarshana Chakra

· Indra gave his thunderbolt

· Varuna gave his conch

· Agni gave his spear

· Yama gave his staff of time

The Goddess waged a fierce battle with Mahishasura. Mahishasura would become a buffalo, then a lion, then an elephant, but the Goddess pursued him in every form."

The Maharshi detailed the battle:

"When Mahishasura became a buffalo, the Goddess rained sharp arrows upon him. When he became a lion, the Goddess struck him with her sword. When he became an elephant, the Goddess slew him with her axe. Finally, when Mahishasura again became a buffalo, the Goddess pinned his neck under her foot and pierced his heart with her trident. Mahishasura was slain, and the gods regained heaven."

The gods, overjoyed, praised the Goddess:

"Victory to you, O Mahadevi! Victory to you, O Jagadamba! Victory to you, O remover of sorrows! O all-pervading Shiva, bestower of auspicious fruits!

You are the ordainer of all, worshipped by Hari and Hara! I have come to your refuge alone, O Mother Ambika!"

Pleased with the praise, the Goddess told the gods to ask for a boon. The gods simply prayed: "O Jagadamba, whenever we call upon you, may you come and remove our sufferings."

The Maharshi explained to Kaashvi:

"Child, Mahishasura is the symbol of our ego. This ego sometimes shows foolishness as a buffalo, sometimes exhibits pride as a lion, sometimes displays power as an elephant. The various powers of the Goddess are the divine capabilities within us. When we awaken these capabilities, our ego is automatically destroyed."

The Maharshi began the third narrative:

"There were two demon brothers named Shumbha and Nishumbha, even more powerful than Mahishasura. They too took control of all three worlds. All the gods worshipped Maa Bhavani, and then the manifestation of Lord Shri Shakti occurred. The Goddess's form was supremely beautiful. And simultaneously, all the powers of the gods also manifested:

Chamunda: The power of Devi Chandi

Brahmani: The power of Lord Brahma

Vaishnavi: The power of Lord Vishnu

Maheshwari: The power of Lord Shiva

Kaumari: The power of Lord Kartikeya

Varahi: The power of Lord Varaha

Indrani: The power of Lord Indra

Vinayaki: The power of Lord Ganesha

Narasimhi: The power of Lord Narasimha

Once, when the Goddess was wandering on the Himalayas, Shumbha's messengers saw her extraordinary beauty and reported it to Shumbha and Nishumbha."

The Maharshi dramatically presented the messenger's message:

"O Goddess! Both Shumbha and Nishumbha are lords of the demons, masters of all worlds. They wish to see you, therefore, O Goddess! Proceed to the abode of the demon lords. This message is sent by the demon kings."

The Goddess replied with a smile, 'I have taken a vow that I will marry only the one who defeats me in battle. Therefore, Shumbha and Nishumbha must come here and conquer me.'

Hearing this, Shumbha and Nishumbha sent a vast army led by Chanda and Munda. With a single roar of her lion, the Goddess annihilated the army. Then when Chanda and Munda approached, Kali manifested from the Goddess's wrath and slew them. Thereupon the Goddess declared, 'From now on, you shall be known as Chamunda.'

Then came Raktabija, from every drop of whose blood a new demon was born. Chamunda began drinking his blood while the Goddess struck him. Thus Raktabija was slain.

Finally, Shumbha and Nishumbha themselves came for battle. The Goddess slew Nishumbha, then fought a fierce battle with Shumbha."

Shumbha says to the Goddess: "Taking so many divine powers, what strength do you show? If you have courage, come alone."

The Maharshi intoned the Goddess's words in a solemn voice: "In this world, there is only I; who else is there? Behold these powers in the form of gods, who have sprung from my own essence. All gods are gathered here, yet I am alone. Today on the battlefield, alone will I slay you."

Saying this, the Goddess slew Shumbha.

The gods again praised the Goddess:

"O Narayani, salutations to you. You are the bestower of all auspiciousness, the embodiment of good fortune. You are the benevolent Shiva, the fulfiller of all desires. You are the giver of refuge, the three-eyed one, the fair one. O Narayani, we bow to you again and again."

"In the end, even the ego of knowledge is not right; its destruction too is necessary."

Maharshi Advaitanand completed the narrative. Tears filled Kaashvi's eyes, but now they were not tears of sorrow, they were tears of joy. On her face was a unique peace and determination.

"My child Kaashvi," the Maharshi said, "this is the tale of the Devi Mahatmya. King Surath and the merchant Samadhi, upon hearing this story, worshipped Mahamaya. In the end, the Goddess granted King Surath the boon of an eternal kingdom, and he became the Manu of the next manvantara. And to the merchant Samadhi, the Goddess gave the knowledge of liberation. Ultimately, both attained moksha."

"But remember, this is not merely a story of external demons." The Maharshi explained further: "When ignorance and attachment overshadow the mind, consciousness drowns in darkness. Mahakali destroyed that darkness. By slaying demons like Madhu and Kaitabha, she taught that as long as tamas (inertia, attachment) is not eliminated, the rise of knowledge is impossible.

Then, when the mind becomes active, there arises within it ego, desire, and lust for power. Mahishasura was the symbol of this rajas quality. Mahalakshmi slew him, giving the message: perform action, but let there be no 'I' in the action. The end of ego is the beginning of dharma.

Finally, when the mind becomes pure, the subtlest ego takes birth within it: 'I am wise, I am holy.' Mahasaraswati destroyed Shumbha and Nishumbha, breaking even this pride of sattva quality. She taught that renunciation of knowledge too is necessary, because ego, in whatever form, is the final bond on the path of liberation."

The Maharshi continued: "The Goddess is that divine power which resides within us. When we invoke that power, it annihilates all our inner demons. Therefore, daughter, if you seek peace in love, first bring peace to your mind. Tomorrow is Pratipada, the auspicious festival of Navratri begins tomorrow. Call upon the Goddess within you; she will remove all your doubts."

Kaashvi touched the Maharshi's feet. "Gurudev, you have dispelled all my doubts. Now I understand that true power does not lie outside, it resides within us."

"I had thought my struggle was with my father, with my love, and with society's rules. But now I understand that my real struggle is with the ignorance and ego within myself."

The Maharshi smiled. "Your name is Kaashvi, which means 'one who illuminates.' Just as the city of Kashi dispels the darkness of ignorance, so too shall you spread the light of this wisdom."

Sunset was descending upon the Vindhyachal, and the temple bells rang out for the evening arati. The tale of the Goddess was complete, but its light had awakened forever in Kaashvi's heart.

Kaashvi resolved that she would remain in this temple of the mind, serving the Goddess and imparting this wisdom to other seekers. She now understood that true love and true liberation lay not in breaking external bonds, but in freeing oneself from internal bonds.

Maharshi Advaitanand blessed her: "Child, now your true sadhana begins. Go and embody this wisdom in your life."

And thus began the new chapter of Kaashvi's life, a chapter that tells the immortal saga of love, courage, and faith.

6: penance

It was the time of dawn. The gentle breeze descending from the Vindhyachal hills flowed through the temple courtyard, caressing the blooming flowers. The first ray of the sun had painted the mountain peaks with a golden radiance. The sweet chirping of birds infused the atmosphere with the music of devotion. Princess Kaashvi, having bathed and donned white garments, entered the sanctum sanctorum of the temple.

She established a sacred kalash before the idol of Maa Vindhyavasini. The kalash was filled with water from the Ganga, on which mango leaves floated. She adorned the temple pavilion with mango leaves and flowers, and lit the first lamp. The flame of the lamp pierced the darkness of the temple, spreading a divine aura.

Tears filled Kaashvi's eyes, but these were not tears of sorrow, they were tears of resolve. Joining her palms, she took a vow: "For nine days, I will partake only of water and meditate upon the Mother. May this penance of mine be for the welfare of all those who walk the path of love and truth."

She praised Maa Shailaputri and prayed for the success of her penance:

"O Daughter of the Mountain, Shailaputri, embodiment of unshakeable devotion!

Grant me that same steadfastness within,

That my mind may never waver.

Just as the mountain remains unmoved in every storm,

So may I stand firm in every trial.

O Himalayan daughter, may my heart remain

As unwavering as you,

Free from all temptations,

And ever fixed upon your feet alone."

Maharshi Advaitanand stood at a distance, observing this scene. A smile of contentment was on his face.

He knew that Kaashvi's spiritual journey had begun. He quietly entered the temple and said: "My child, this form of Maa Shailaputri teaches us how important stability and firm resolve are in life. Just as a mountain remains unmoved in every season, so must a seeker remain steadfast in their goal in every circumstance."

Kaashvi asked humbly, "Gurudev, will this vow of mine truly reach the Mother?"

The Maharshi replied affectionately, "Child, when a vow is taken with selfless intention, it surely bears fruit. Your resolve has been strengthened further by the purity of your heart."

The second day's sunrise arrived. Kaashvi had remained in the temple all night. The lamp's light fell upon her face, making her countenance appear divine. She was meditating upon Maa Brahmacharini, the embodiment of penance, restraint, and faith.

Maharshi Advaitanand said as he entered, "Child, Maa Brahmacharini performed severe penance to attain Lord Shiva. She meditated for thousands of years, first subsisting on fruits and flowers, then only on leaves. This penance bestowed upon her extraordinary inner strength."

Kaashvi asked, "Gurudev, is it impossible to attain inner strength without penance?"

The Maharshi smiled, "One who conquers oneself can attain the Mother. Penance is not external action, but inner resolve. This vow of yours is itself your penance. Penance means mastering the senses, controlling the mind, and awakening the soul."

Kaashvi, reflecting deeply, said, "Gurudev, is love also a form of penance? Can my love for Madhav be part of my penance?"

The Maharshi replied with delight, "Child, pure love is the greatest penance. When love is selfless, it becomes devotion. Your love is not just part of your penance, it is its foundation."

Kaashvi praised Maa Brahmacharini:

"O Maa Brahmacharini, presiding deity of penance, grant me inner strength.

Let my tears become an offering, and my silence become a chant.

Just as you renounced food and water to perform penance,

So may I renounce worldly attachments.

O wearer of the akshamala, may every breath of my life

Become your remembrance,

May every heartbeat become your chant,

And may every moment be passed in your devotion."

On the third day, the sweet sound of bells resonated in the temple. The temple flag fluttered in the wind. Kaashvi meditated upon Maa Chandraghanta, who destroys fear.

Today, a strange restlessness was in Kaashvi's mind. She remembered her father, who had compelled her to leave the palace. She began to be troubled by fear of society's harsh traditions. Fear of public shame started to haunt her. Had she made the right decision? Could she truly walk this path?

The Maharshi perceived her state of mind. He said, "Child, Maa Chandraghanta's name comes from the half-moon adorning her forehead. This half-moon signifies that in life, both joy and sorrow, light and darkness, coexist. Fear is merely a thought of the mind, not truth."

Kaashvi said, "Gurudev, I am afraid that perhaps this path of mine is wrong. Perhaps I am making a mistake by renouncing everything for my love?"

The Maharshi explained, "Child, fear arises when we forget the power within us. Maa Chandraghanta's bell symbolizes that divine sound which reminds us of our inner strength. When you hear this divine sound within yourself, all fears will automatically dissolve."

Taking a deep breath, Kaashvi praised Maa Chandraghanta:

"Maa Chandraghanta, dispel the darkness of my inner being.

Let that sacred bell sound within me that speaks only truth.

Just as the sound of your bell removes fear,

So may my heart's beat become courage.

O ten-armed one, let my ten senses

Be engaged in your devotion,

Remove all my doubts,

And make my mind fearless."

On the fourth day, a wonderful transformation was visible on Kaashvi's face. Despite her fast, there was a smile on her lips. Like Maa Kushmanda, she was feeling the essence of creation.

The Maharshi said with delight, "Today, the image of Maa Kushmanda is visible on your face. Kushmanda means 'Ku' (small), 'Ushma' (energy), and 'Anda' (cosmic egg), the Goddess who created the vast universe from a small energy."

Kaashvi spoke, "Gurudev, today I feel that this struggle of mine is also a creation of a new life, a new consciousness. Just as Maa Kushmanda created the universe, I am creating my life anew."

The Maharshi affirmed, "Devotion begins with tears, but ends in light. Your tears are now transforming into light. Your heart is now filling with creative energy."

Kaashvi praised Maa Kushmanda:

"O Maa Kushmanda, initiator of creation,

Kindle a new light within my heart.

Just as you spread light in darkness,

So dispel the darkness of my life.

O embodiment of creation, bring forth

New hope in my life,

Infuse new energy,

And usher in new love."

On the fifth day, sitting before the Mother's idol, Kaashvi experienced deep peace within for the first time. She was meditating upon Skandamata, the mother of Kartikeya.

She thought, "The Mother too is the mother of a son, just as a woman's heart is filled with love. Motherhood is the nature of all women, whether goddess or human."

The Maharshi, understanding her thoughts, said, "The form of Skandamata symbolizes compassion and affection. When you become filled with the maternal feeling, all anger, envy, and hatred within you automatically cease."

Compassion began to shine in Kaashvi's eyes. Instead of anger toward her father, she began to feel pity. She understood that he too was bound by society's constraints. She felt concern for Madhav, was he safe? Did he miss her too?

The Maharshi said, "Child, the compassion awakening in your heart today is an important stage in your spiritual journey. Compassion is the bridge that connects man to divinity."

Kaashvi praised Maa Skandamata:

"Maa Skandamata, grant me the sweet compassion of motherhood.

Fill my heart with an ocean of compassion.

Just as you gave affection to Skanda,

So may I give affection to all beings.

O mother of Kartikeya, awaken within me

That love which is equal for all,

That love which is selfless,

And that compassion which is all-pervading."

On the sixth day, Kaashvi looked toward the sky, courage welled up from within. Seeing birds flying in the sky, she felt her freedom. She resolved that she would no longer fear for her love and truth.

The Maharshi said joyfully, "Today, Katyayani has awakened within you. Maa Katyayani slew Mahishasura. That Mahishasura is the symbol of the fear and doubt within you."

Kaashvi spoke, "Gurudev, today I feel I can overcome every obstacle. My love is my strength, my faith is my sword. I know my path is difficult, but now I have no fear."

The Maharshi blessed her, "You are truly blessed, child. You have recognized the Goddess within yourself. Maa Katyayani was born in the ashram of Maharshi Katyayana, and today she has been born in your heart."

Kaashvi praised Maa Katyayani:

"O Katyayani, goddess of valor, give me the strength to protect dharma.

Let my tears now become a sword.

Just as you slew Mahishasura,

So may I slay the ego within me.

O slayer of Mahishasura, destroy

All doubts within me,

Annihilate all fears,

And remove all weaknesses."

The seventh night was intense. A storm raged outside. The lamp kept extinguishing repeatedly, but the lamp of Kaashvi's heart remained blazing. She was meditating upon Maa Kalaratri, who puts an end to fear.

The Maharshi came to the temple and said, "Maa Kalaratri's form is fearsome, but she bestows auspicious results for devotees. She destroys the darkness of ignorance and spreads the light of knowledge."

Kaashi said, "Gurudev, today I feel that all my fears have ended. Whatever I lost was external. What I have gained is internal. My love, my faith, my devotion, these are my true wealth."

The Maharshi said with happiness, "This is indeed the effect of Maa Kalaratri. She destroys not external darkness, but inner darkness. When inner darkness ends, external darkness automatically transforms into light."

Kaashvi praised Maa Kalaratri:

"O Maa Kalaratri, devour the darkness within me.

Turn my fear to dust beneath your feet.

Just as you destroyed Raktabija,

So destroy my negative qualities.

O fierce-formed one, burn away

All impurities within me,

Eliminate all afflictions,

And cut all bonds."

On the eighth day, Kaashvi's face held an extraordinary radiance, her eyes a gentle softness. She bathed, donned white garments, and offered flowers to Maa Mahagauri. Her heart had now become pristine.

The Maharshi observed and said, "Today you appear like Maa Mahagauri herself. Mahagauri means one of extremely fair complexion. When the mind becomes free from all sins and impurities, it becomes as pure and divine as Mahagauri."

Kaashvi spoke, "Gurudev, today I feel that my mind has become as pure as the water of the holy Ganga. All difficulties, all sorrows have been washed away. For whatever I have lost, there is now no regret in my heart."

The Maharshi blessed her, "In this purity of yours resides the Mother. When the heart becomes pure, the Goddess herself comes to dwell in it. This purity of yours has invited the Mother to manifest before you."

Kaashvi praised Maa Mahagauri:

"O Mahagauri in white garments, wash away the impurities within me.

Now, purified, I will chant only your name.

Just as your form is immaculate,

So may my mind become immaculate.

O fair-complexioned one, wash away

All the filth of my life,

Remove all sins,

And dispel all impurities."

It was the night of Navami. A gentle breeze was blowing. The temple flag fluttered. Kaashvi was in deep meditation before the Mother's idol. Her mind was completely calm and concentrated.

"O Mother!

I know neither mantra nor tantra,

I do not know the methods of your worship,

Nor have I understood the depths of meditation.

I only know this much,

True happiness lies only at your feet,

And all sorrows dissolve only in your refuge.

O Mother!

On this earth, you have many virtuous sons, daughters, and devotees,

But perhaps there is none as ignorant and humble as me.

And the one who protects such a humble one is only you, Mother.

Therefore, O Ambe!

Give this weak one a place at your feet,

Grant me your vision,

For a son may be an unworthy son,

But a mother is never an unworthy mother.

O Mother!

Throughout my life, I have taken only your name,

I have known no one but you.

If you do not accept me, who else will?

You alone are my mother, you alone are my support.

O Jagadamba!

I am ignorant, I am sinful, I am fallen, but I am yours alone.

You are the purifier of the fallen, full of compassion, full of mercy.

I have no knowledge of vows, nor of penance,

I do not know the ways of sadhana,

I rest only on your love and your grace.

Therefore, O Maa Jagadamba!

Bless me,

Grant me your vision,

Cradle me in your lap,

Just as a mother comforts her frightened child."

Then a wondrous event occurred. A divine light appeared in the temple. The radiance was so intense that Kaashvi's eyes automatically closed. When she opened her eyes, Maa Vindhyavasini stood before her, with a gentle smile, filled with compassion.

The Mother's form was indescribable. In her hands were the gestures of fearlessness and boon-giving. On her face was infinite compassion and love. The Mother said in a tender voice: "Daughter, your love is pure. You have performed penance more purifying than water. The purity of your heart and the firmness of your resolve have compelled me to appear."

The Mother blessed her:

"I grant you these boons, you shall have unbroken good fortune, your love shall surely find you, your son shall be radiant and righteous, and at the end of your life, you shall attain my abode. This sacrifice and penance of yours shall not go in vain. You shall not only attain your love, but your courage shall inspire countless women. Your name shall be inscribed in history in golden letters."

Kaashvi bowed to the earth. Her tears now were not of pain, but of liberation. She said, "Mother, I desire only that my life be spent in your service. I want nothing, only your love."

The Mother gave the final blessing: "So be it. May your wish be fulfilled." And she became invisible.

Maharshi Advaitanand came and raised Kaashvi. "Child, your sadhana is now complete. You have not only received the Mother's blessing, but have awakened the Goddess within yourself."

Kaashvi said with a smile, "Gurudev, now I understand that the Mother is not somewhere outside, she resides within us. Our struggle itself is our sadhana, and our courage itself is our worship."

The Maharshi said, "From today, you are no longer merely Kaashvi. From today, you have become the devotee of Siddhidatri, who has attained all siddhis."

And thus, Kaashvi's Navratri sadhana was complete. She had not only received the Mother's blessing, but had awakened within herself a new power, a new consciousness, and a new vision. Now she knew that her path was clear and her journey was just beginning, a journey that would give light not only to her, but to many others.

The temple bells began to ring, and nature itself, witnessing this sacred moment, filled the atmosphere with a wonderful peace and joy. Kaashvi closed her eyes, enshrining the Mother's divine vision in her heart, and knew that from now on she was not alone, the Mother was always with her.

7: The Divine Union

Many months had now passed since Princess Kaashvi had come to the ancient temple of Maa Vindhyavasini. Time had moved at its own pace, sometimes slow, sometimes swift, but ever-flowing. In the proximity of Maharshi Advaitanand, she had attained the realization of Brahman, known the infinity of the soul, and glimpsed the ultimate truth.

Her mind was now steady, calm, and unwavering, like the depths of the ocean where no storm can reach. She had come to understand that even the pinnacle of knowledge remains incomplete if it lacks love. After touching the supreme heights of Brahmajnana, she realized that love is the thread that connects the individual soul to the Supreme Soul.

Yet somewhere within, a tender void still remained, the memory of Madhav. That memory existed in her heart as a sweet pain. The Mother had promised, "You shall surely attain your love." Kaashvi was in waiting. She knew not which moment the Mother's boon would bear fruit. She knew that divine words are never false, but when does the human heart's restlessness ever embrace patience?

It was the season of Sharad. Nature had adorned herself. The sky was clear, the air cool, and the earth lush green. On that day, the sky was particularly pristine, as if nature herself awaited some divine occurrence.

As evening fell, the moon revealed its face in the eastern sky. It was full, as if a stream of nectar was flowing from it. The soft rays of moonlight filtered through the forest leaves and scattered upon the earth, as if the heavens were showering nectar.

Maharshi Advaitanand called Kaashvi. "My child, today is Sharad Purnima. This night is supremely sacred. The moon's rays contain nectar. Bring water from the lake. I shall perform a special worship today."

Kaashvi bowed her head in assent. She lifted a golden kalash and, leaving the temple, walked toward the lake.

The scene at the lake was wondrous. In the moonlight, the water gleamed like silver. Lotuses had bloomed, and upon them, dewdrops sparkled like pearls. The fragrance of champaka and bela flowers mingled in the breeze, touching the mind with sweetness.

Kaashvi placed the kalash at the edge and gently stepped into the water. The touch of the water was cool and pleasant. She had just bent down to collect water when suddenly she felt that someone was seated upon a tree. A strange sensation seized her heart.

She looked up, on a guava tree sat a young man. Moonlight fell upon his face, lending him a divine aura.

That face, that same intense gaze, that same humble smile, it was none other than Madhav.

For an instant, time stood still. Kaashvi's breath seemed to stop. Her eyes could not believe. Is this real? Is this not a dream?

Madhav too was stunned seeing her. His eyes widened. Seeing Princess Kaashvi in this forest, by this lake, he was speechless.

Kaashvi composed herself and called out in a soft voice: "Madhav!"

The call reached Madhav's ears, and he jolted back to reality. He quickly descended from the tree and came down.

They drew near each other. No words, no questions, only two hearts, now united by the Mother's boon. The years of separation dissolved in a single breath. Time seemed to pause.

Madhav gazed at Kaashvi. In his eyes were astonishment, love, and wonder. "Princess... is it truly you? Is this not a dream?"

Tears welled up in Kaashvi's eyes. "Yes, Madhav, this is no dream. It is I, your Kaashvi."

They embraced each other. This embrace was not merely the union of bodies; it was the union of souls. The moonlight showered nectar upon them, as if Maa Bhavani herself was bestowing her blessings.

After some time, both sat by the lake's edge. Madhav spoke: "Princess, I thought I would never meet you again. After that day, so much happened..."

His voice became emotional. "The king issued a proclamation against me, that I had enticed you, violated the kingdom's honor. Orders were given for my imprisonment. A decree was issued that if I were found within the boundaries of Vindhyagadh, I would be punished with death."

Pain surfaced in Kaashvi's eyes. "O God! I knew nothing of this."

Madhav continued, "But the elder Mahesh Das sent me away overnight. He said, 'Son, flee. Go wherever your destiny takes you.' Since then, I wandered in this forest and ultimately took refuge here, surviving on fruits and flowers, trusting in Maa Bhavani."

Kaashvi wiped her tears and said, "And I too had taken refuge in the Mother's temple. That day when you told me we must part, my heart broke. I left the palace and came straight to this temple. Maharshi Advaitanand taught me the path of devotion and knowledge. He explained to me that love is not a sin, but the greatest sadhana. And the Mother herself appeared and said, 'You shall surely attain your love.' Today I understand that this was that day. The Mother's word has proven true."

They both looked toward the sky, the full moon seemed to smile at that moment, as if heaven itself was blessing this love. A divine peace pervaded all around. The leaves of the trees rustled softly, as if nature was singing the song of this union.

Madhav held Kaashvi's hand. "Kaashvi, how these years passed without you, I myself do not know. Each day felt like a thousand years and passed in memories of you. Each night I dreamed of you."

Kaashvi said in a sweet voice, "I too was waiting for you. The Maharshi taught me that true love tests one's patience. And today, that test is complete."

They sat for a long time, narrating their stories to each other. Every word held love, every sentence held faith. The moonlight continuously showered nectar upon them, as if the moon god himself was witnessing this union.

Following her guru's instructions, Kaashvi placed the pot of cool water in the temple. Maharshi was absorbed in meditation, so she did not deem it appropriate to discuss this matter with him then.

The next morning, Kaashvi brought Madhav to Maharshi Advaitanand. The Maharshi was absorbed in his morning sadhana. When he saw them both together, a gentle smile bloomed on his face, as if he had known everything beforehand.

"Come, my child," the Maharshi said. "The Mother's words are never false. I knew this moment would come one day."

Kaashvi said humbly, "Gurudev, this is Madhav. By the Mother's grace, we have been united."

The Maharshi blessed Madhav. "Son, you too have endured great hardships. But see, today those very hardships have brought you to this divine union."

The Maharshi said in a solemn voice: "This love is not merely worldly; it is the union of souls. When two souls are destined for each other, the entire universe arranges the means for their meeting."

The Maharshi decided that their marriage should be performed that day. "Today is extremely auspicious. This time is excellent for a divine union."

The temple courtyard was decorated. Garlands of flowers were strung. Lamps were lit. The Maharshi himself undertook the role of priest. The time for the wedding arrived. Kaashvi and Madhav stood before the idol of Maa Vindhyavasini. The Maharshi began the chanting of mantras. Every mantra held a divine energy, every word carried a spiritual vibration. The Maharshi's voice echoed in the temple.

Kaashvi and Madhav placed garlands upon each other. This was not merely a garland of flowers; it was a garland of love and faith.

The Maharshi said, "From today, you are not merely husband and wife, but two pillars of devotion and love upon which the balance of creation rests. May this love of yours become a source of inspiration not only for yourselves but for the entire world."

At the conclusion of the wedding ceremony, a wondrous event occurred. A divine light radiated from the idol of Maa Vindhyavasini. This light was so brilliant yet gentle that everyone's eyes were dazzled.

The Maharshi said in a joyful voice, "Behold! The Mother herself has come to bless them."

Both looked toward the idol. It seemed as though the idol had come alive. On the Mother's face was a divine smile, and in her eyes, infinite compassion and love.

The Maharshi said, "The Mother has accepted your love. This marriage is not merely human, it is divine."

At night, when all was quiet, both sat outside the temple. The river flowed with a sweet murmur, the moon smiled, and the stars twinkled.

Holding Kaashvi's hand, Madhav said, "Kaashvi, now I desire nothing, only that this moment become immortal. The life I lived without you was merely existence. Today, I am truly alive."

Kaashvi replied in a sweet voice, "Madhav, love found in the Mother's shelter never fades. This love is beyond time and boundaries. This is Vindhyagatha, where love born of devotion was purified by knowledge and made immortal by truth."

Madhav said, "Kaashvi, do you know? After you left the palace, the king repented. He sent people to search for me, but by then I had already come here."

Compassion welled up in Kaashvi's eyes. "Father, he too was bound by his duties. I do not blame him. Perhaps it was the Mother's will that we pass through this path."

Madhav asked, "What will we do now, Kaashvi? Will you return to the palace?"

Kaashvi said with firmness, "No, Madhav, my palace is here. This temple of the Mother, this forest, this nature, this is my kingdom. And you are my king."

Madhav smiled at her words and said, "Then we shall remain here. I will serve the temple, and you will remain absorbed in the Mother's devotion. Our life shall pass in simplicity and love."

Kaashvi bowed her head calmly. "Yes, this is best. We need not the dominion of any external power, but the sovereignty of the kingdom within us."

The next day, Maharshi Advaitanand called them both. "My children, now your union is complete. But remember, this union is not of bodies alone, it is of souls. You must both help elevate each other's souls even further."

The Maharshi continued, "The true meaning of love is this: to give each other freedom, to aid each other's growth. You both have endured great hardships, but now the time has come for you to become a source of inspiration for others."

Kaashvi said humbly, "Gurudev, we shall remain under your guidance. We need your blessings at this new stage of our life."

The Maharshi blessed them, "So be it. May the Mother protect you, and may your love ever continue to flourish."

Thus, Kaashvi and Madhav's life entered a new chapter. The temple where Kaashvi once lived alone now became abode to love and affection. Madhav engaged himself in serving the temple, and Kaashvi in her worship of the Mother.

Their love was not merely for themselves. It became a message of love for the entire forest, all of nature, the whole world. Birds sang songs of their love, trees blessed them, and the river carried away the story of their love in its flow.

8: The Boon

After the divine marriage of Kaashvi and Madhav at the temple of Maa Vindhyavasini, their life had entered a new chapter. That temple courtyard where once only the bells of devotion had rung now began to resonate with the sweet sounds of love and affection.

Maharshi Advaitanand arranged for a small hut to be built for them within the temple premises. This hut was simple, yet so enriched with love and devotion that no palace could rival its abundance. Its walls were of mud, its roof of thatch, yet a divine warmth pervaded it.

At dawn, Kaashvi would go to the temple for the Mother's worship, while Madhav would engage himself in the temple's service. He would sweep the courtyard, tend to the flowering plants, and help prepare prasad for the devotees.

One evening, as they both sat in the temple courtyard, Kaashvi said in a sweet voice, "Madhav, do you ever feel any regret for what we left behind?"

Madhav took a deep breath and replied, "Kaashvi, the splendor of palaces, ornaments of gold and silver, royal luxuries, I have forgotten all of this. The peace and contentment I have found with you in this simple hut cannot be found in any palace."

Kaashvi smiled. "I think the same. The joy found at the Mother's feet is not in any worldly pleasure."

Soon, however, a new challenge arose. For their sustenance at the temple, money was needed for food and other necessities. Madhav only served the temple, and their financial situation was becoming increasingly difficult day by day.

One evening, when Kaashvi saw Madhav sitting in a worried state, she asked, "My lord, why are you so troubled? What is the matter?"

Madhav admitted the truth. "Beloved, we have very little money left. I am thinking of doing some work so that we can sustain ourselves."

Kaashvi said wisely, "You are right. We have devotion and love, but for food and other necessities, we do need money."

The next day, Madhav made plans for the neighboring kingdom. He would gather fruits, flowers, and wood from the forest and go to the neighboring kingdom to sell them. Initially, this work was difficult, but gradually he gained proficiency in it.

One day, when Madhav returned from the neighboring kingdom, he was excited. "Beloved, today I sold my goods at good prices. Now we can be carefree for a few days."

Kaashvi said happily, "By the Mother's grace, everything is becoming possible. But my lord, you should not have to endure too much hardship."

Madhav said firmly, "No, beloved. You left the splendor of the royal palace for me. Why can I not do this small labor for you?"

A few months later, an auspicious event occurred. Kaashvi became pregnant. Hearing this news, Madhav's joy knew no bounds. He fell at Kaashvi's feet and said, "Beloved, the Mother's boon is coming true! She had said that your son would be radiant and righteous."

Tears came to Kaashvi's eyes. "Yes, my lord, every word of the Mother proves true. I have seen the Mother in a dream. She was telling me that this son will bring welfare to the entire Vindhya region."

During the days of pregnancy, Kaashvi and Madhav's love deepened even further. Madhav remained engaged in Kaashvi's service day and night. He would bring nourishing food for her, take care of her health, and take her on nature walks for entertainment.

One day, as Kaashvi sat absorbed in meditation at the temple, she had a divine experience. Maa Vindhyavasini appeared to her and said, "Daughter, your son will be great. He is my supreme devotee. I entrust you with the responsibility of his upbringing. May you be blessed."

Kaashvi rose from meditation and told this to Madhav. Tears of pride and wonder came to Madhav's eyes. "Beloved, we are so blessed that the Mother has given us the opportunity to give birth to this great soul."

Meanwhile, Maharshi Advaitanand decided to enter deep samadhi. One day, he called Kaashvi and Madhav and said, "My children, now I must enter deep samadhi. No one knows how long this samadhi will last. During this period, I will disconnect from the external world."

Kaashvi asked with concern, "Gurudev, will you be able to remain without food and water for such a long time?"

The Maharshi smiled. "Child, in the state of samadhi, this body is sustained not by food and water but by divine energy. Do not worry. The responsibility of caring for the temple and both of you now rests upon you."

Madhav said humbly, "Gurudev, we will follow your command. You may enter samadhi without any worry."

The next day, the Maharshi entered samadhi. He went into a secluded chamber of the temple and immersed himself in deep meditation. Kaashvi and Madhav would regularly go outside his chamber and pray, but the Maharshi remained completely absorbed in samadhi.

Upon the completion of nine months, Kaashvi gave birth to a radiant son. At birth itself, the child's face held an extraordinary brilliance. His eyes were large and wise, as if he knew all the mysteries of the universe.

Madhav took the newborn in his arms and shed tears. "Beloved, look! The Mother's boon has manifested. This child is not ordinary."

Kaashvi said in a weak voice, "Yes, my lord, at the time of birth, I saw the Mother in a dream. She was blessing this child."

The child's naming ceremony was performed. The Maharshi could not be present himself due to being in samadhi, but Kaashvi and Madhav named the child "Aaditya", radiant like the sun.

Aaditya gradually began to grow. He was different from ordinary children. When other children would play and run about, Aaditya would sit amidst nature and become absorbed in meditation. His questions were so profound that Kaashvi and Madhav would be astonished.

One day, Aaditya asked, "Mother, where does this bird come from? And where does this river go? Did Maa Vindhyavasini create everything?"

Kaashvi was amazed. Such profound questions in the mind of such a small child!

One day, Madhav had gone to the neighboring kingdom to sell goods. By chance, a minister of King Mahendra Pratap had also come to that same marketplace. The minister recognized Madhav.

The minister's name was Shubhranshu. He was kind and just. Seeing Madhav, he called him near. "Madhav, is that you? The lover of Princess Kaashvi?"

Madhav became frightened. "Sir, please forgive me. I"

Shubhranshu said with a smile, "Do not fear, Madhav. I will not harm you. I have heard that Princess Kaashvi is also with you. Is this true?"

Madhav admitted the truth. "Yes, sir, Kaashvi is with me. We live at the temple of Maa Vindhyavasini."

Shubhranshu said seriously, "Madhav, King Mahendra Pratap does not know of this. But may I meet the princess once? I wish to ensure her safety."

Madhav, trusting him, said, "You may come, sir, but please ensure that the king does not get wind of this."

The next day, Shubhranshu arrived at the temple in ordinary dress. When he saw Kaashvi, he was speechless. Kaashvi's form had become even more divine and radiant than before. And when he saw Aaditya, his eyes filled with emotion.

"Princess!" Shubhranshu said emotionally, "You are safe! And this child?"

Kaashvi said with a smile, "Shubhranshu ji, this is my son Aaditya. The boon of Maa Vindhyavasini."

Shubhranshu went near Aaditya. The child looked at him fearlessly. Shubhranshu said, "This child is not ordinary. There is a wonderful radiance in his eyes."

Kaashvi narrated the entire story to Shubhranshu, how the Mother had given them the boon, how Maharshi Advaitanand had performed their marriage, and how Aaditya was born.

Shubhranshu took a deep breath and said, "Princess, I will convey this news to the king. The king feels deep remorse. He has remembered you many times."

Kaashvi said humbly, "Shubhranshu ji, please tell Father that I am well and have no complaints."

Shubhranshu returned and told everything to King Mahendra Pratap. When the king heard that his daughter was safe and that he also had a grandson, he became emotional.

"Kaashvi, my daughter!" Tears flowed from the king's eyes.

The king felt deep remorse. That night, he could not sleep. He had a vision of Maa Bhavani in a dream. The Mother said, "O King, your daughter's son shall be the heir to your kingdom. Place him on the throne. This is my command."

At dawn, the king summoned Shubhranshu. "Shubhranshu, I will go to the Vindhyavasini temple today itself. I must meet my daughter and grandson."

Shubhranshu nodded happily. "Maharaj, this is extremely auspicious news."

King Mahendra Pratap, in ordinary dress, without any royal pomp, arrived alone at the temple. When he saw Kaashvi, his eyes filled with tears.

Kaashvi was playing with Aaditya in the temple courtyard. When she saw the king, she froze. "Pita-shri!"

Without saying anything, the king fell at Kaashvi's feet and sought forgiveness. "Kaashvi, forgive me. I wronged you."

Kaashvi immediately raised him. "Pita-shri, do not say such things. Whatever you did, you did according to your dharma. I have no complaint."

Just then, Aaditya came there. He looked at the king fearlessly. The king lifted Aaditya into his arms. "This... this is my grandson?"

Kaashvi said with a smile, "Yes, Pita-shri, this is Aaditya. The boon of Maa Vindhyavasini."

The king embraced Aaditya. Aaditya also touched the king with affection. It seemed as if an invisible bond existed between them.

At that moment, Maharshi Advaitanand's period of samadhi was complete. After five years of deep samadhi, he arose from meditation. When he came out of his chamber, he saw the king with Kaashvi and Aaditya.

A divine light shone on the Maharshi's face. He smiled and said, "Welcome, Maharaj. I knew that one day you would surely come."

The king touched the Maharshi's feet. "Maharshi, by your blessings, I have realized my mistake."

The Maharshi said, "Maharaj, this was the Mother's will. Everything is her divine play."

The Maharshi asked Kaashvi, Madhav, and the king to sit and deliberate. The Maharshi said, "Maharaj, now you must decide. Should Kaashvi and Madhav remain here or return to the royal palace?"

The king said, "Maharshi, I desire that Kaashvi and Madhav return to the palace. Let Aaditya be made the heir to the kingdom."

Kaashvi said humbly, "Pita-shri, we are very happy in this forest and temple. This is our true home."

Madhav also agreed. "Maharaj, we have no need for royal splendor."

But the Maharshi explained, "Child, this is not merely about your happiness. It is about the welfare of the kingdom. Aaditya must become the heir to the kingdom, for this is the Mother's will. And you must accept the responsibility of the kingdom's prosperity, for this is your dharma."

The Maharshi continued, "The Mother's boon had to be fulfilled. Madhav, there is another secret concerning you."

The Maharshi said in a solemn voice, "Madhav, you are not merely a gardener's disciple. You were also born in a royal dynasty."

All were astonished. Madhav said in disbelief, "Maharshi, how is this possible?"

The Maharshi narrated the story: "Many years ago, the king of a neighboring kingdom had a son. At his birth itself, astrologers had prophesied that this child would grow up to become a great and just emperor. But it was written in his destiny that he would have to spend some years in the forest, undergoing difficult penance and struggle.

There was celebration in the kingdom, but at that time, clouds of conspiracy gathered. The king's deceitful and ambitious minister, who himself dreamed of sitting on the throne, became frightened by that prophecy. One night, through treachery and betrayal, he murdered the king and seized the kingdom for himself.

When the queen received this news, her heart trembled with grief and fear. She knew that the next target would be her child, Madhav. To protect her son, she entrusted him to her trusted confidant, the gardener Mahesh Das, and said, 'Take this child to a safe place where the eyes of these conspirators cannot reach.'

Mahesh Das accepted the queen's command. In the darkness of night, carrying the infant Madhav in his arms, he fled through dense forests. After wandering for days, he settled in Vindhyagadh, where he raised Madhav. Meanwhile, when the queen learned that the minister had sent soldiers after them, knowing that escape was no longer possible, she decided to become Sati with her husband. In the flames of her pyre, it seemed as if the compassion of the entire kingdom and the fire of injustice burned together.

Since then, Madhav grew up in the forest hermitage of Vindhyagadh with that elderly gardener."

Madhav was stunned. "So Mahesh Kaka, he was not my father?"

The Maharshi nodded. "He was your guardian. By the boon of Maa Bhavani, you were destined to become king. When the Mother protects someone, what can anyone do to harm them?"

Now everyone understood that all of this was the Mother's divine play. The Maharshi, giving farewell to Kaashvi, said, "Child, now you must go. Always walk on the path of dharma. This kingdom needs your and Madhav's guidance."

Kaashvi and Madhav sought the Maharshi's blessings. Both husband and wife offered their final prayers at the temple and departed for the kingdom.

King Mahendra Pratap, filled with remorse, decided to renounce the world. "I have made many mistakes in my life. Now I will spend the rest of my life in devotion."

A grand ceremony was held at the royal palace of Vindhyagadh. Madhav and Kaashvi were crowned. Aaditya was declared the crown prince. The entire populace welcomed the new king and queen.

Madhav and Kaashvi began to rule righteously. They made justice, compassion, and love the foundation of the kingdom. Special arrangements were made for Aaditya's education and training, so that he might become an ideal ruler in the future.

The boon of Maa Vindhyavasini was completely fulfilled. Kaashvi attained her love, she received unbroken good fortune, her son became radiant and righteous, and ultimately, the path to the Mother's abode was also paved for her.

This saga of Vindhyagadh became a sacred legend over time, a saga in which love crossed all obstacles, devotion faced all adversities, and truth ultimately triumphed. The love of Kaashvi and Madhav was no longer theirs alone; it became a source of inspiration for the entire Vindhya region. And even today, when anyone goes to that ancient temple in the Vindhyachal, their problems are certainly resolved.

www.ingramcontent.com/pod-product-compliance
Lightning Source LLC
LaVergne TN
LVHW090421210926
848480LV00002B/645
* 9 7 9 8 2 3 3 6 9 2 6 7 3 *